LITTLE MISS STUBBORN

Roger Har

Original concept by
Roger Hargreaves

EGMONT

Little Miss Stubborn was, as you might imagine, extraordinarily stubborn.

Once she had made her mind up, there was no unmaking it.

If she decided to go out, she went out.

Even when it was pouring with rain!

One Sunday, when it wasn't raining, she decided to take the bus to Mr Strong's house.

Why?

Because she had run out of eggs.

And, as everybody knows, Mr Strong always has lots of eggs.

As the bus arrived, Mr Nosey walked by.

Being nosey, he couldn't help asking, "Where are you going, Little Miss Stubborn?"

"To Mr Strong's house," she said.

"But this bus doesn't go anywhere near there!"

But Little Miss Stubborn took the bus anyway.

And you won't be surprised to hear that it didn't go anywhere near Mr Strong's house.

It went to Coldland.

A country where it is so cold that everybody has
a cold all year round.

"What a charming place!" she said, shivering and
trying to look as if she had really planned on coming
to Coldland in the first place.

Which of course she hadn't.

As you know.

She ran along a path to keep warm.

"ATISHOO!" somebody sneezed all of a sudden.

It was Mr Sneeze.

"If I were you," he warned, "I wouldn't take …
ATISHOO! that path. It's icy! ATISHOO!"

"I'll take it if I want to!" snorted Little Miss Stubborn.

And she followed the path.

But, can you guess what happened?

WHOOOOOOSH!

She slipped on the ice!

"That was fun!" said Little Miss Stubborn.

But of course it wasn't.

She came to a fork in the path.

"I shall go this way," she said, taking the right-hand path.

"You're making a big mistake!" said a worm, popping his head through the snow.

"This way isn't safe."

"Don't be silly!" cried Little Miss Stubborn, and started off down the path.

She should have listened to the worm!

Before she had gone very far an avalanche of snowballs fell on top of her!

One of the snowballs rolled off the path and rolled and rolled down a very steep hill.

And, inside it, Little Miss Stubborn rolled and rolled down the very steep hill as well.

The snowball rolled a very long way, all the way into a different country, where it melted.

As luck would have it, Little Miss Stubborn found herself outside Mr Strong's front door.

She was soaked to the skin.

"My goodness! You're wet through!" said Mr Strong.

"Quick, come in and dry yourself before you catch a cold."

"I don't catch colds," said Little Miss Stubborn. "Anyway, I've come for some eggs. Out of my way!"

"That's no way to behave," said Mr Strong.

"Rubbish!" snorted Little Miss Stubborn.

Still wet through, she marched into Mr Strong's kitchen.

Without a please or a thank you, she helped herself to a large bowl of eggs.

"You could at least ask," said Mr Strong.

"ATISHOO!" sneezed Little Miss Stubborn.

"I told you you'd catch a cold," said Mr Strong.

"I don't catch colds," said Little Miss Stubborn, and sneezed again, "ATISHOO!"

She was so hungry by this time that, there and then, she made herself an enormous omelette.

It was gigantic.

It was so big that it won't even fit on the page!

Then she began to eat her enormous, gigantic omelette.

And the more she ate, the more worried Mr Strong became.

"You'll make yourself ill," he said.

"Fiddlesticks," snorted Little Miss Stubborn and, because she was who she was, she finished that enormous, gigantic omelette.

And there is not much more to add.

Other than now you know how extraordinarily stubborn Little Miss Stubborn is!

Stubborn to the very end … the very end of this story.